Dangerous Animals

Written by
Bobbie Whitcombe

CHECKERBOARD PRESS

NEW YORK

In this book you can read about dangerous animals and what makes them dangerous.

Some animals are dangerous because they are big and fierce. Tigers are the largest of the big cats. Look at this **tiger**'s sharp teeth. It is hunting for animals such as deer, wild pigs and cattle. An old or injured tiger may attack humans.

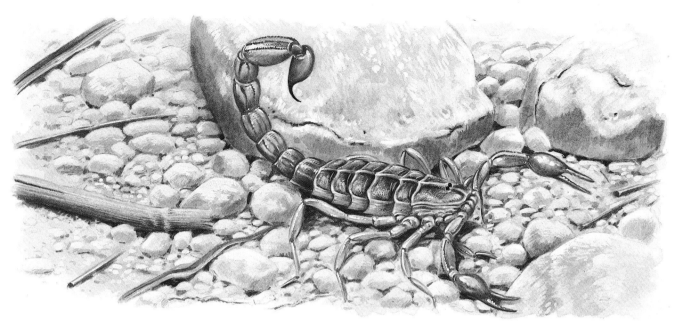

Some small creatures can be as dangerous as larger ones. Look at the way this **scorpion** holds its tail. The sharp sting stabs into its prey and poisons it. The poison from some African scorpions can kill a person within hours.

The large spider is a female **black widow spider**. She is very dangerous. Her bite is poisonous and can sometimes be fatal. The male is harmless, though.

The animals here are meat-eaters. They may attack people if they are hungry.

Crocodiles live in hot countries. They lurk in marshes and rivers, waiting to catch animals that come to drink. With most of its body under the water, this crocodile looks like a floating log. Look at its powerful jaws.

Look at the size of this **anaconda**! This South American snake lurks in the water for an animal to come to the water's edge. It kills by wrapping itself around its victim and crushing it.

Lionesses are hard to see in the long, dry grass. They hunt for meat for their families. They will stalk a deer or zebra and then attack swiftly. When they are too old to catch other animals, lions may attack people.

These animals do not attack people for food. But they may be dangerous if they think they are in danger themselves.

Grizzly bears live in the North American forests. They feed mainly on fish, fruit and leaves. When it stands upright, the grizzly is taller than a man. It is very strong. It can kill large animals with one blow of its paw.

The **cassowary** is
a bird which cannot
fly. It can run fast
and has strong legs.
It lashes out with
these if people get
too close. Its
powerful kick can
kill a person.

Gorillas are the biggest of the apes.
They look dangerous but they are gentle.
They attack only if someone frightens
them. An angry male will beat his chest,
roar and may charge at a stranger.

Most animals are dangerous when they are looking after their babies.

This **Cape buffalo** will charge at anyone getting near her calf. She fights fiercely and uses her long horns and sharp hooves. The lioness had better keep well clear of those pointed horns!

The **harpy eagle** is guarding its nest. Look at its feet. Each one is bigger than your hand. It uses its sharp claws and beak to attack anything that comes near its chicks.

The **giant panda** looks like a big cuddly toy, but it can be dangerous. The adult is big and heavy. It has strong paws with sharp claws. A female panda will hit out to protect her young cub. She even keeps the male away.

Many animals become dangerous if they are hurt or frightened.

The **rhinoceros** is a shy creature with poor eyesight. But if it is startled by a noise or sudden movement, it may attack with its long horn. It can run fast and will even charge at cars!

Elephants are gentle animals. They can be trained to help people in their work. Look at these **Indian elephants** moving huge logs. There are some people who shoot elephants for their ivory tusks. A wounded elephant will charge at a hunter.

Some animals are dangerous when there is a large group of them together.

Wolves hunt in packs. They can kill an animal as big as a moose. They attack again and again until the animal is weak. Then they kill it. When they are hungry, wolves may attack people.

Hyenas hunt in packs too. They often attack a wounded animal, like this wildebeest. They can crush the biggest bones with their strong jaws. The vultures will feed on the leftovers.

Look at the sharp
teeth of these **piranha**
fish. They live in
South American rivers.
They are small, but
a shoal of them can
eat a big animal.

Insects can be very harmful to people,
especially when there are hundreds of
millions of them in a swarm together.
Locusts travel great distances eating
everything growing near them. They
destroy all the crops for miles. Then
people and animals may starve.

There are some deadly creatures in the sea.

This is a **hammerhead shark**. It has a very
good sense of smell. Can you see its
nostrils, set wide apart on its head?
It waves its head from side to side as it
hunts for its prey. If it smells blood,
it swims fast to attack with its
sharp teeth.

Look at the long
tentacles of this
Portuguese man o'war
jellyfish. This
creature can give
a painful sting
to humans.

The Pacific **octopus** has eight arms. Each
arm can be up to 5 metres (16 feet) long.
Rows of strong suckers on its arms grip
its prey, which it kills with
a fierce bite. It could
be dangerous for a
swimmer to be caught
by these arms!

Some creatures can be harmful to people because they carry disease.

The **vampire bat** is found in South America. It can pass disease from animals to humans by biting them. Can you see its teeth?

Mosquitoes live near ponds and marshes. Some kinds of mosquito carry diseases like malaria and yellow fever. They pass the disease by biting people.

Rats live all over the world wherever there are stores of food. Look what these black rats have done! Because they sometimes live in dirty places, rats can carry disease. Then the food they have touched makes people ill.

Flies eat rotten food which is full of germs. They can carry the germs to food that humans then eat. The germs can make humans ill.

Some snakes are poisonous. They bite their victim and inject venom into it with sharp fangs.

This African **boomslang** is a tree snake. It lies hidden in the branches and strikes suddenly at its prey. Its venom can kill a person.

The **Indian cobra**'s bite can be fatal too. It rears up like this before striking. As well as biting, some cobras can spit poison at their victim.

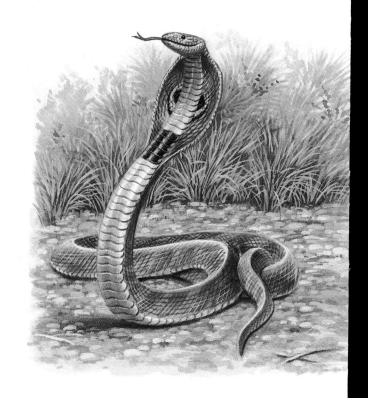

There is another very dangerous animal. These creatures hunt and kill many other animals. They are changing the world around us. They cut down forests and spill deadly poisons onto the land and into rivers and lakes. They are very clever. They have invented the deadliest of weapons. This creature has the power to destroy the land and all the animals on it. The most dangerous animal is **man.**

Do you recognise these animals?
The names at the bottom of the page will help.
What makes these animals dangerous?